This book belongs to:

_____

My pets' names are:

_____

My favorite animals are:

_____

Mimi and Maty to the Rescue!

Book 3

C.C. the Parakeet

Flies the Coop!

Written by Brooke Smith

Illustrated by Alli Arnold

Better World Kids Books
New York

Sky Pony Press
New York

For Kelly and Mimi - as always.
For Maty's extraordinaire Mom, Lynne.
And for Julie - for believing in Mimi + Maty + Me!

— Brooke

For all the kids who love animals and books - you rock!

— Alli

Sky Pony Press books may be purchased in bulk at special discounts for sales promotion, corporate gifts, fund-raising, or educational purposes. Special editions can also be created to specifications. For details, contact the Special Sales Department, Sky Pony Press, 307 West 36th Street, 11th Floor, New York, NY 10018 or info@skyhorsepublishing.com.

Sky Pony® is a registered trademark of Skyhorse Publishing, Inc.®, a Delaware corporation.

Visit our website at www.skyponypress.com.

10 9 8 7 6 5 4 3 2 1

Manufactured in China, May 2014
This product conforms to CPSIA 2008

Library of Congress Cataloging-in-Publication Data is available on file.

Cover design by Karina Reck
Cover illustrations credit Alli Arnold

Print ISBN: 978-1-62914-620-1
Ebook ISBN: 978-1-63220-219-2

CHAPTER ONE

Today was Maty's and my first day of second grade.

Well, not really. It was *my* first day of second grade. Maty had to stay at home.

Maty's my amazing three-legged rescue dog and my very best friend.

I wish Maty could come to school with me. I miss her so much when we're apart.

And since Maty and I are official animal rescuers, it makes it super hard. You never know when we might be called into action!

OFFICIAL
Animal Rescuers
Mimi + Maty
Call us: 389-2424

I didn't want Maty to be sad when I left for school this morning, so I did a bunch of special things to make her feel better.

I fluffed her doggy bed,

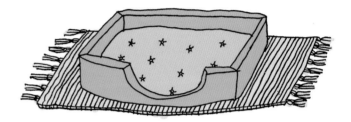

put her favorite toys all around the house,

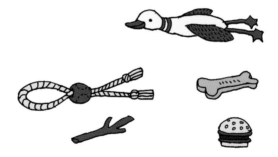

taped a drawing of us on her doggy door,

and set my alarm clock for 2:45
(the time school gets out).

Mom said as soon as the alarm went off, Maty ran to the front door and started to bark. Mom grabbed her leash and they headed to school to pick me up. (Yep, Maty's one smart pooch alright.)

On the way home, we stopped at Goodies Ice Cream Parlor to celebrate my first day of second grade.

Mom got a hot fudge sundae.

Extra hot fudge
(hold the nuts.)

I ordered the boomerang banana split.

And Maty had her usual—a doggy delicious ice cream sandwich.

When we sat down to eat our goodies, Mom asked how my first day of school went.

I told her it was a thumbs up/thumbs down kind of day.

Thumbs up:

I have my favorite teacher in the whole school—Ms. Weber!

Ms. Weber

She loves animals and has the most beautiful Golden Retriever named Aspen, and a super furry cat named Dot. There's a photo of them on her desk.

Plus, Ms. Weber loves volunteering at the animal shelter. Dad and I saw her there a bunch this summer.

Thumbs down:

Being without Maty for six hours. Boy, did I miss her.

Thumbs up:

There's a new girl in class named Emma. She's sort of shy, but seems really nice. She wore a super cute T-shirt with a bird on it and said it looks just like her pet parakeet C. C.—who she loves a lot.

Emma

(I think I'm going to like this girl.)

Big thumbs down:

I sit *right* behind Icky Vicky. Her huge, gigantic hairdo has gotten even bigger over the summer, and I can barely see the blackboard.

But the best thumbs up of all is that tomorrow is Ms. Weber's famous second grade "Bring Your Pet to School Day"! Everyone in the whole school knows about Ms. Weber's pet day and looks forward to it every year.

Last year a boy named Big Jim surprised
everyone by bringing the smallest pet ever—a tiny
black ant named Andy.

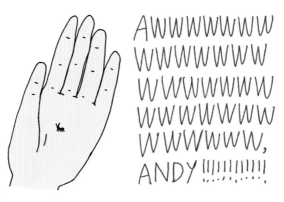

AWWWWWW
WWWWWWW
WWWWWWW
WWWWWWW
WWWWWW,
ANDY!!!!!!!!!!

And the year before, Cora (the teacup pig) fell
asleep in Ms. Weber's coffee cup.

awwwwwwwww
wwwwwwwww
wwwwwwwww
little cora!
(so, so, so cute!!!)

22

But no pet in the history of Edgewood Elementary could ever be as awesome as my Maty.

After ice cream, we headed home so I could do my homework. We're supposed to write down all the things that make our pets special so we can share them with the class.

I got out my rescue notebook and started in:

My dog Maty (a.k.a. my best friend)

- I adopted Maty from the animal shelter.

- She only has three legs– but it doesn't slow her down one bit.

- She plays Frisbee, skis, hikes, and even skateboards!

- My mom and dad are crazy about her!

- Maty and I are official animal rescuers, because we love to help animals.

- We also just LOVE animals (except snakes– Maty's scared of snakes).

- My Maty makes me smile every single day.

I put my notebook in my backpack, along with a bunch of other animal rescue stuff (including the new walkie-talkies my dad got me this summer)

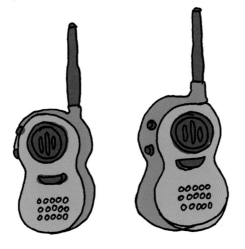

and decided I better start getting Maty ready for the big day.

I gave her a bath.

I brushed her teeth.

BRUSH
BRUSH
BRUSH

(Now her breath smells like peppermint.)

And I put a new bandana around her neck. She looks awesome!

I can't wait until tomorrow. I know Maty's going to find a way to make it a *double thumbs up* kind of day.

CHAPTER TWO

The hallway in front of Ms. Weber's classroom looked just like a mini zoo.

Hayden brought his dwarf hamster, Harley.

Chelsea was holding a fishbowl and giggling as her goldfish Bella swam around in circles.

Annie cuddled her adorable kitten, Slippers (who looks just like a fuzzy slipper).

Christopher had his pet cricket, Sebastian, tucked inside his pocket.

And Emma was carrying her birdcage, which was covered with a blanket so you couldn't see her bird (but you could hear her sweet tweets coming from the cage).

Tweet! Tweet! Tweet! Tweet! Tweet! Tweet! Tweet! Tweet!

Maty sat right by my side with a smile on her face a mile wide. She couldn't wait to meet Ms. Weber and my whole second grade class.

Ms. Weber opened the door and asked us all to come in and take our seats. As Maty and I walked by Icky Vicky's desk, I made the mistake of asking her if she'd brought a pet to school today.

"You mean a *pest*, not a pet, don't you?" she said in a super meanie voice.

"If you ask me, today should be called 'Bring Your *Pest* to School Day,'" she said as she looked straight at Maty.

"Don't you dare call Maty a pest . . ." I started to say just as Ms. Weber told us all to look up at the blackboard.

She'd written down the order that we'd be sharing our pets and said we needed to get started. We had a big, fun day ahead of us.

Emma and her parakeet were first on the list, and Maty and I were second.

1. Emma
2. Mimi
3. Christopher
4. Chelsea
5. Annie
6. Hayden

Emma carried her birdcage to the front of the room and put it on Ms. Weber's desk. She took off the blanket . . . and there was the cutest parakeet I've ever seen!

She was blue with little dots around her neck and a tiny orange beak.

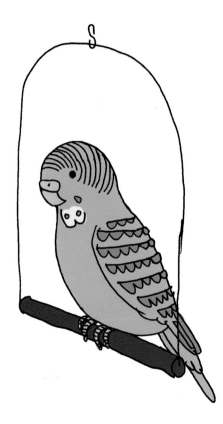

Emma said she named her C. C. after her grandma and got her when she was just a baby bird. (Imagine how cute a baby parakeet must be?)

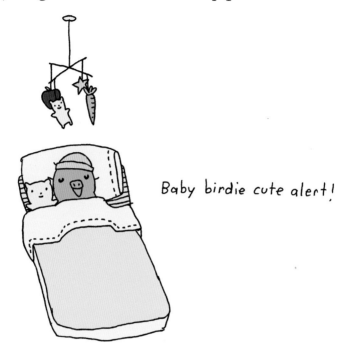

Baby birdie cute alert!

Ms. Weber asked Emma if she could please talk a little louder to make sure everyone in the back could hear her. (I think Emma's shy, plus being the new girl probably makes her even extra nervous.)

But I could tell she really loved C. C. and wanted us all to know how great she was.

I guess C. C. has tons of toys:

She has a Ferris wheel
that she spins on;

a Hula-Hoop that she
jumps through;

and a
birdie bowling
game that she
plays over and
over again.

She can blow
bubbles in her water
dish.

And she even
plays peek-a-boo.

(Wow! Parakeets are awesome birds.)

And one of C. C.'s favorite things to do is to fly around Emma's bedroom and then come in for a landing on Emma's shoulder to get her tummy rubbed.

A couple kids asked if they could see C. C. fly. Emma said sure and took C. C. out of the cage and put her on her finger.

C. C. flew right off, no problemo—but our second grade classroom has one thing that Emma's bedroom does *not* have . . .

a giant Icky Vicky hairdo sticking straight up in the sky!

And sure enough, when C. C. was flying back to Emma, she flew right into Vicky's pile of hair. (I wonder if she thought it might make a good nest?)

Well, you can only imagine what happened next. Icky Vicky screamed like only Icky Vicky can scream. (I'm pretty sure all of Edgewood Elementary could hear her.)

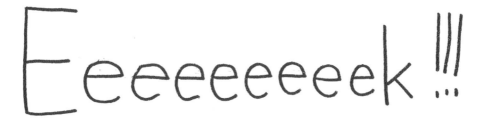

"Get this squawking, feathered pest out of my beautiful hair *now!*"

Emma froze at the front of the classroom. She couldn't believe what was happening.

Ms. Weber ran over and tried to detangle little C. C. from Vicky's hair.

When C. C. finally got free, she flew straight for an open window on the far side of the classroom.

(I think she'd had enough, the poor little birdie. She definitely picked the wrong head of hair to fly into.)

Icky Vicky went screaming down the hallway, straight for the school nurse.

"Bird cooties, bird cooties, someone help me! I have bird cooties!"

And now C. C. the parakeet was somewhere in the wild blue yonder—and it was up to Maty and me to jump into action and find her!

CHAPTER THREE

And jump into action we did.

Maty and I walked up to the front of the classroom and told Ms. Weber that we are official animal rescuers.

George yelled from the back of the room that we're 100 percent the real deal. He said we found his friend Otto's pet rat, Roger, and saved the day big time.

Roger

HOME SWEET HOME

I asked Ms. Weber if Emma, Maty, and I could go outside and look around for C. C. She might have just flown into a tree out on the playground.

She could be here...

... or here

..., or here

...or here

... or here

Ms. Weber said that she's glad to have animal rescuers in her class this year.

And she said sure, we could head out to the playground and take a look around. Mr. Connor and his third grade class were out on recess. Maybe some of his kids could even help.

I told her that Maty and I usually work alone or like to handpick our team. So we could sure use George. He's already been part of a successful rescue mission and knows how Maty and I work.

George was *so* excited.

I grabbed my notebook and backpack (official animal rescuers are always prepared) and headed out to the playground.

Maty looked in the bushes.

George checked out the playground equipment.

And Emma and I looked high up in the trees, calling C. C.'s name over and over again.

But there was no sign of C. C. Nothing. Nada. No sweet blue parakeet anywhere.

I decided I better sit down and start taking some notes:

Notes to me:

- Today is: "Bring Your Pet to School Day."
- And it's also: "A Parakeet Flew Out the School Window Day."
- The parakeet's name is C.C. and she belongs to the new girl, Emma (who seems really nice).
- There's no sign of C.C. on the playground.
- This could be a tough rescue because the sky is a very BIG place to find a very tiny bird.

If I'm going to rescue a bird, I need to think like a bird. And lucky for us, one person who knows tons about our fine, feathered friends is . . .

my mom! She's a birder extraordinaire.

My mom.

I told George he needed to hold down the fort at school. I gave him a walkie-talkie (he thought it was super cool) and said to let us know right away if there's any sign of C. C.

Then Emma, Maty, and I went to the office and called my mom. She said she'd come right away to pick us up, and to tell Emma that she knows lots about parakeets and is sure everything's going to be A-OK.

Boy, do I have a great mom, or what?

CHAPTER FOUR

As soon as we got home, Mom headed straight up to the attic to get her special bird box. My mom has loved birds ever since she was a kid and has a box of books and other birding stuff that she's kept forever.

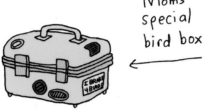

Mom's special bird box ←

Emma, Maty, and I went to the kitchen and helped ourselves to some banana bread.

(YUMMY)

I decided I'd better ask Emma some questions about C. C. Maybe she has some information that might help us find her.

I took out my notebook and started writing stuff down:

C.C. Info:

· Emma says C.C. is a shy, sweet bird.

· She's been sad and a little lonely since they've moved.

· She misses her:
  - old house
  - old bedroom
  - old friends
  - old school

(Hmm, sounds like Emma might be talking about herself, not C.C.)

My mom finally found her box and inside was
just what she was looking for . . .

her parakeet book.

Bobby
Bird
←

Mom loves to tell the story of her parakeet,
Bobby Bird, who she had when she was a little girl.

One day, when Bobby Bird was flying around her house, someone left the toilet seat up and Bobby Bird flew right into the toilet!

He was A-OK—he just needed to be dried off and given some extra TLC. But Mom still remembers how sad she was that something bad almost happened to him.

Phew! Close call!

I said I sure hope Emma and C. C. have the same happy ending.

Emma started reading Mom's book. I asked her to tell me some parakeet facts that might give us some clues and I'd write them down in my notebook:

PARAKEET FACTS

(from Mom's special book)

1. When frightened, a parakeet will fly towards the light – like an open window. (Just like C.C. did at school!)

2. When lost in the wild parakeets will get very thirsty and will search everywhere for water.

3. Parakeets love shiny things.

4. Snakes and birds of prey can hurt them. (No wonder Maty doesn't like snakes.)

5. Parakeets' eyesight is more powerful than humans' (that's why we need ~~bion~~ binoculars).

6. Parakeets poop and pee at the same time.

7. They sleep a lot, mostly at night. You should cover their cage to make them feel safe.

8. If a parakeet throws-up on you (Yikes!) it means she thinks you're family and is trying to feed you.

9. Parakeets recognize their owner's voice and will come when they hear it. If they're scared you should use a soothing voice to call them.

10. Parakeets YELP when they're scared and WARBLE when they're happy. Emma says it sounds like a cat purring.

All of a sudden, Maty started to bark and came running into the kitchen with my backpack.

My walkie-talkie was beeping and Maty had heard it. I got it out as fast as I could. It was George, and he said that he had great news!

"I found C.C,!"

After school, George was getting onto the school bus when out of the corner of his eye he saw C. C. perched on the mirror of the bus.

3. Parakeets love shiny things.

She was just sitting there, looking at herself.

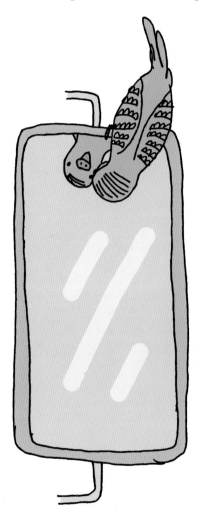

George was going to pick her up and keep her safe until we got there.

Mom said she'd zoom us back to school pronto. She told me to take her binoculars—they might come in handy.

I had my fingers crossed (and Maty crossed her paws) that C. C. would sit tight—and not take flight. Because help is on the way!

CHAPTER FIVE

As soon as Mom dropped us off, Emma, Maty, and I ran straight to the school bus.

We saw George at the front of the line, but yikes! No sign of C. C.

Where's C. C. ???

George said she'd flown the coop . . . again!

I guess right after he'd gotten off the walkie-talkie with me, C. C. saw something even shinier than the mirror.

Icky Vicky and her groupies (girls who act icky, so they can be just like Vicky) were standing at the back of the bus line holding their back-to-school, shiny blue water bottles.

Not only were the bottles super shiny, but they were full of water and C. C. was probably really getting thirsty.

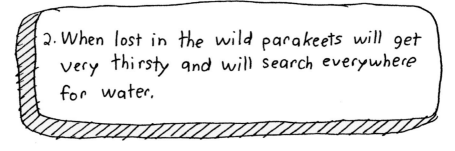

2. When lost in the wild parakeets will get very thirsty and will search everywhere for water.

George said C. C. flew to the back of the line and tried to land on each of the blingy bottles.

He thinks C. C. remembered Vicky, because she pecked at her water bottle the most.

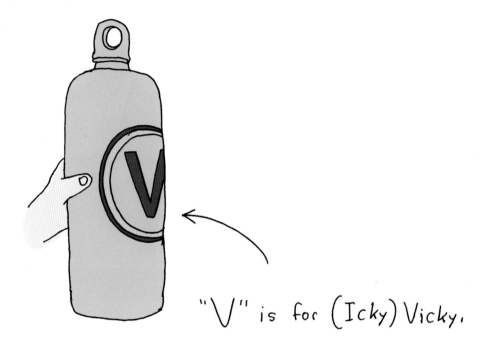

"V" is for (Icky) Vicky.

All at once, Icky Vicky and her buddies freaked out and threw their bottles straight up into the air!

And C. C. flew right up with them . . . up, up, up into the tip top of the trees, and she just kept on flying.

Now George is afraid that after being scared *twice* by crazy, meanie girls that C. C. might never want to come back down.

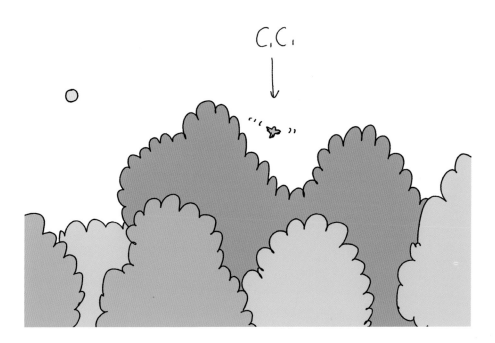

Emma looked heartbroken, so Maty went over
and snuggled next to her (Maty's "hope you feel
better" hug).

I told Emma not to worry. We're going to find
C. C. if it's the last thing we do.
If C. C.'s headed for the treetops, then so are we.
Tree House Park, here we come!

CHAPTER SIX

Tree House Park is the coolest park in town, and it's right in our neighborhood.

The tree house sits in the middle of a forest. It has ropes, a circular staircase, and a deck that wraps all the way around it.

Since C. C. was too scared to come down from the trees, we would have to go up to find her . . . and a tree house was our best bet.

We climbed to the top and went out on the deck. It seemed like you could see forever.

The sun was starting to set, and I could tell Emma was getting sad.

She said that every night, just before bedtime, she covers C. C.'s cage and sings her a special lullaby to help her fall asleep. She just couldn't imagine not doing that tonight.

75

Well, as soon as Maty heard the word *lullaby*
she started to howl and howl and howl—super loud!

When Maty howls, she thinks she's singing.
She howls to the radio, when I sing in the shower,
and even when people play music at the dog park.

But this time, her howls were so loud and we were so high up that I was sure the whole town could hear her.

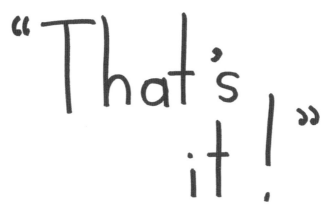

"That's it!"

I shouted. "That's what Maty's trying to tell us!"

Maty wanted Emma to sing her lullaby from the top of the tree house so C. C. could hear her.

9. Parakeets recognize their owner's voice and will come when they hear it. If they're scared you should use a soothing voice to call them.

I thought Maty's idea was a great one, but I have to say, I was a little worried. A dog's loud howl is *a lot* different than a shy girl's soft voice. But it was definitely worth a try. (And let's face it, Maty is the smartest rescue dog ever.)

"Emma, Maty's right," I said. "You need to sing your lullaby, and you need to sing it *now!* As loud as you can."

Emma said she was too nervous. She's never sung it in front of anyone but C. C. I told her to just give it a try—to close her eyes and think of C. C.

Well, when Emma started to sing, I could barely believe my ears. . . .

Shy Emma, with the quiet, tiny voice, had the most beautiful singing voice I've ever heard.

It was so beautiful and lovely that the words and notes seemed to float through the air and over the treetops.

"Hush, little C.C., don't tweet a word.
It's time to go to bed my tiny, tired bird.

I know you want to fly and play
but you need to go to sleep, it's been a long day.

So close your eyes and have no fear,
when you wake up I'll be right here."

"Keep singing, Emma, keep singing," I said. "You're doing great."

And sure enough, from far off on the horizon, I could see a little speck flying towards us.

I grabbed the binoculars . . .

and yelled "Hip, hip, hooray!" It was C. C. and she was headed our way!

And right after Emma sang the last line of her lullaby,

"I love you so much, my sweet C. C. dear."

C. C. the parakeet swooped in and landed on Emma's shoulder—right where she belonged.

CHAPTER SEVEN

Emma tucked C. C. in her sweater, and we all walked back to my house.

Mom was so excited to see us! We put C. C. back in her cage, and she warbled up a storm.

warble warble warble warble
warble warble warble warble
warble war rble warble
warble wo le warble
warble w ble warble
warble w ble warble
warble w le warble
warble w ble warble
warble warble warble warble
warble warble wa ble warble
warble warble wa ble warble
warble warble warble warble

She was sure one happy bird!

85

Emma's dad came to pick her up and he thanked us for everything. He was glad Emma had such nice, new friends.

Maty and I ate dinner and headed up to bed. It had been one long, *amazing* day.

I kept a light on, because I needed to finish up my rescue notebook with a huge happy ending.

HUGE Happy Ending and Stuff!:

- We found C.C. the parakeet!

- George helped us, Icky Vicky screamed A LOT, and my new walkie-talkies really came in handy.

- Emma sang C.C. a lullaby from a treehouse, and C.C. flew back just as the sun was setting. (It was Maty's idea!)

• Now Emma feels lucky to have new friends that love animals and who helped her find her lost little bird.
(She thinks we're awesome animal rescuers, by the way!)

☆ ☆ ☆ ☆ ☆ ☆ ☆

• And mom had so much fun telling us about Bobby Bird that she wants to get another parakeet! Maty loves that idea (and so do I!),

I told Maty that I'm going to write her a lullaby, just like Emma did for C. C. That way, I can sing her to sleep every night.

I already know how it's going to start:

"Hush, little Maty, don't bark a word,
You're the best dog in the whole wide world."

Maty smiled and closed her eyes.

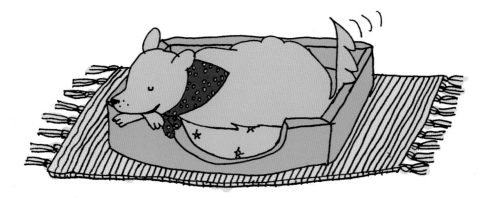

(Wow! Lullabies really do work.)

She's one tired rescue dog. But don't worry all you animals out there . . . after a good nights sleep, we'll be back in action!

Lost or hurt animals have no fear. Mimi and Maty are here!

Meet the real...

Mimi has always loved animals. When she was seven years old, she started a rescue notebook so she could keep track of all the animals she's helped: butterflies, birds, and chipmunks . . . even a rainbow trout!

When Mimi was eleven years old, she wanted to help feed the dogs and cats at her local shelter in Bend, Oregon, so she created the website Freekibble.com. Freekibble has now fed over 11 million meals to homeless pets at shelters and rescues across the country.

Maty is now the Humane Society of Central Oregon's goodwill ambassador. She visits schools and groups, teaching people about animal safety and showcasing the many abilities of a disabled dog. Maty is also the first three-legged dog to qualify and compete in two Skyhoundz World Canine Disc Dog Championships. Way to go, Maty!

Mimi and Maty met through their work at the animal shelter and have been special friends ever since. With their big hearts, Mimi and Maty continue to inspire others to help, care for, and love animals.

Maty at school!

About the Author:

Brooke Smith is Mimi's mom. She has always wanted
to write a book inspired by Mimi's big heart and
all the fun she has helping animals. With this book,
Brooke hopes to get other kids excited to help all of
the four- and three-legged creatures that need them.

About the Illustrator:

Alli Arnold is never without a pen and paper. Her first illustration was published when she was just seven years old, and she has gone on to illustrate for such clients as the *New York Times* and Bergdorf Goodman. Alli's little dog, Nino, likes to chase pigeons and squirrels. To see more of Alli's drawings, go to www.alliarnold.com.